MILES OF SMILES

MILES OF SMILES

Kids Pick the Funniest Poems, Book #3

Edited by Bruce Lansky

Illustrated by Stephen Carpenter

Scholastic Inc.
New York Toronto London Auckland Sydney
Mexico City New Delhi Hong Kong

ISBN 0-439-08211-0

12 11 10 9 8 7 6 5 4 3   9/9 0 1 2 3 4/0

Printed in the U.S.A.   23

First Scholastic printing, January 1999

ACKNOWLEDGMENTS

We would like to thank the following teachers and their students
for helping us select the poems for this book:

Marcy Anderson, Dell Rapids Elementary; Mark Benthall, Lakeway
Elementary; Kathy Budahl, L. B. Williams Elementary; Monica Chung,
Edgewood School; Bonnie Cox, Kolmar School; Beth Davis, Hough Street
School; Cheryl Esparza, Monroe Elementary; Linda Evans, Longfellow
School; Nancie Gordon, Whispering Pines Elementary; Shirl Herzig,
Groveland Elementary; Jane Hesslein, Sunset Hill Elementary; Kate Hooper,
Pinewood Elementary; Craig Jackson, Withrow Elementary; Ann Johnson,
Christa McAuliffe Elementary; Margaret Kelberer, St. Paul Academy and
Summit School; Sharon Klein, Clardy Elementary; Barbara Knoss, Hanover
School; Maggie Knutson, Orono Middle School; Dale Langer, Milton East
Elementary; Carol Larson, Mississippi Elementary; Steve Muras, Gatewood
Elementary; Elaine Nick, Gracemor Accelerated School; Tessie Oconer,
Fulton Elementary; Connie Parrish, Gertie Bell Rodgers Elementary; Mitzi
Pearlman, Acres Green Elementary; Mary Jane Savaiano, Clara Barton Open
School; Louise Scholnick, Dr. Gilbert Porter Elementary; Timothy Tocher,
George Grant Mason Elementary; Lynette Townsend, Lomarena Elementary;
Cheryl Triefenbach, Lalumier School; Dr. Jory Westbury, Avalon Elementary;
and Jean Wise, Lincoln Elementary.

CONTENTS

Introduction   xi

ME
Born Embarrassed   Bruce Lansky   2
God Gave Out Noses   Anonymous   3
Birthday Wish   Diane ZuHone Shore   4
Too Many Birthdays   Bruce Lansky   5
It's Not My Fault!   Babs Bell Hajdusiewicz   6
Self Centered   Anonymous   7
Do Not Enter   Florence Parry Heide
                                    Roxanne Heide Pierce   8
He'll Pay for This!   David L. Harrison   9
I Love You   Anonymous   10
Short Love Poem   Judith Viorst   11
Captain Soapsuds   Robert Scotellaro   12
Swimming Ool   Kenn Nesbitt   14

PARENTS
Dance Fever   Robert Scotellaro   16
The Skateboard   Willard R. Espy   17
Lost and Not Found   Babs Bell Hajdusiewicz 18
Mother's Chocolate Valentine   Jack Prelutsky   19
The Sleepover   Betsy Franco   20
Before 9 A.M.   Joyce Armor   21
If You Make Me Go to Bed Now   Jeff Moss   22
There Was a Man   Dennis Lee   24

BROTHERS AND SISTERS

My Baby Brother	Bruce Lansky	26
Babies	Jeff Moss	28
My Problem's Worse!	Babs Bell Hajdusiewicz	31
My Brother	Like Havumaki	32
Things I'm Going to Do to My Brother	Joyce Armor	33
My Brother Built a Robot	Jack Prelutsky	34
Potty Trainer	Susan D. Anderson	36
Forgetful	Bruce Lansky	37
For Sale	Shel Silverstein	38

SCHOOL

School Rules	Bruce Lansky	40
No Thanks	Joyce Armor	42
Jasper Jeans	Russ Walsh	43
My Feet	Kenn Nesbitt	44

FOOD

Oops!	Bruce Lansky	46
The Proper Way to Eat	John Frank	48
An "Everything" Pizza	Linda J. Knaus	50
A Balanced Diet	Robert Scotellaro	52
Big Mary	Bill Dodds	53
Powdered Sugar	Sydnie Meltzer Kleinhenz	54
Little Miss Muffet	Bruce Lansky	56
Cockroach Sandwich	Colin McNaughton	57
The Yuckiest Sandwich	Ellen Jackson	58

GROSS OUT

Table Manners	Joan Horton	61
Sound Off!	Susan D. Anderson	62
Beans	Anonymous	63
The Bathroom	Babs Bell Hajdusiewicz	64
Sprinkles	Anonymous	65
The Curse of the Foul-Smelling Armpit	Trevor Harvey	66
I See London	Anonymous	68

TALL TALES

My Robot	Douglas Florian	70
Miss Veronica Blair	Linda J. Knaus	72
Humpty Dumpty's Funeral	Blaine and Hardy VanRy	74
Professor Von Shtoot's Wacky Inventions	Helen Ksypka	76
The Turkey Shot Out of the Oven	Jack Prelutsky	78
One-Shoe Willy	Linda J. Knaus	80
True Story	Shel Silverstein	82

CRITTERS AND CREATURES

Dinosaur Names	Holly Davis	84
My Family of Dinosaurs	Helen Ksypka	85
My New Pet	Bruce Lansky	86
Kangaroos	Kenn Nesbitt	88
Mary's Dumb Lamb	Anonymous	90
Old Hogan's Goat	Anonymous	91
Transylvania Dreaming	Colin McNaughton	92
Hey, Ma, Something's Under My Bed	Joan Horton	94

ALL MIXED UP

Mr. Backward	Douglas Florian	98
A Sense-less Poem	Carey Blyton	99
Empty Headed	Linda J. Knaus	100
Dainty Dottie Dee	Jack Prelutsky	102
The Tattered Billboard	Anonymous	104
Cousin Henrietta's Growing Something On Her Face	Jerry Rosen	106
Credits		108
Title Index		112
Author Index		114

INTRODUCTION

When my kids were in elementary school, I noticed that the poems they liked best were the ones they thought were funny. They'd read them over and over and over again—to anyone who would listen. That's how I got the idea to collect the funniest poems by the funniest poets and put them in a single book.

But how was I going to figure out which poems were the funniest? I decided to test fifteen poems I liked on a fourth-grade class in the same school my kids had attended years before. The kids liked about half of the poems I'd selected. I couldn't wait to test the next batch of poems on another class of students.

The poems those kids helped me select were published in *Kids Pick the Funniest Poems,* a book that was a "hit" from the moment it was published. Its success prompted me to publish another collection of funny poems, *A Bad Case of the Giggles,* which was also very successful. Then followed *No More Homework! No More Tests!, Happy Birthday to Me!,* and now this book.

In the process of testing poems by Shel Silverstein, Jack Prelutsky, Jeff Moss, Judith Viorst, and others on classrooms full of kids, I discovered that the poems that made kids laugh the most often contained a nugget of truth about parents, school, pets, or some other topic important to kids. That's why this book is full of poems that deal with such topics as what really happens at slumber parties, messy bedrooms, gaining revenge on bratty brothers and snooping sisters, the latest fashions, white lies, junk food, and foul-smelling armpits.

I've again teamed up with Stephen Carpenter, the illustrator of the first three collections, with the goal of making the illustrations as funny (or funnier) than the poems. People who've read this book say there's a smile on every page. I hope you agree.

Bruce Lansky

Born Embarrassed

My mom was born in England.
My dad was born in France.
And I was born embarrassed,
because I had no pants.

Bruce Lansky

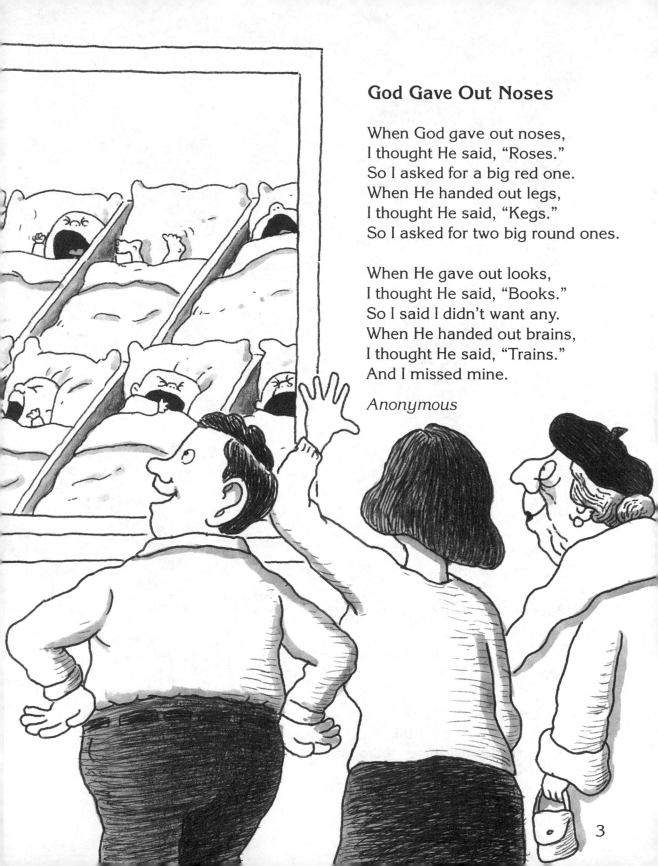

God Gave Out Noses

When God gave out noses,
I thought He said, "Roses."
So I asked for a big red one.
When He handed out legs,
I thought He said, "Kegs."
So I asked for two big round ones.

When He gave out looks,
I thought He said, "Books."
So I said I didn't want any.
When He handed out brains,
I thought He said, "Trains."
And I missed mine.

Anonymous

3

Birthday Wish

When I turned eight I made a wish
I thought was really great.
I wished my birthday came each week—
a year's too long to wait.

Be careful when you make a wish,
it may indeed come true.
Although I'm just in second grade
I'm almost forty-two!

Diane ZuHone Shore

4

Too Many Birthdays

Everyone loves presents.
Everyone loves cake.
But having birthdays every day
would be a big mistake.

We would get so big and round
from eating lots of sweets,
it would be impossible
to get out of our seats.

Bruce Lansky

It's Not My Fault!

I try my best to be polite.
I know what's wrong and what is right.
But sometimes little parts of me
act up and bug my family.

My tongue sticks out.
My knuckles crunch.
My lips make smacking sounds at lunch.
My fingers poke and pinch and pick.
My feet jump out and trip or kick.
My mouth says words that aren't nice—
Today it spit . . . and tattled—twice!

So don't blame me for what they did.
It's not my fault!
I'm just a kid!

Babs Bell Hajdusiewicz

6

Self Centered

I like myself. I think I'm grand.
I go to the movies and hold my hand.
I put my arms around my waist;
when I get fresh I slap my face.

Anonymous

7/15/10

Do Not Enter

Warning
Do Not Enter
Stop
Wrong Way
Beware
Danger
Do Not Trespass
Caution
Don't You Dare

I taped the signs onto the door—
I thought that's all I'd need.

My brother came in anyway—
He hasn't learned to read.

*—Florence Parry Heide and
Roxanne Heide Pierce*

8

He'll Pay for This!

Here I stand, forlorn and bare,
My brother hid my underwear,
I cannot find them anywhere,
So close the door!
It's rude to stare!

David L. Harrison

I Love You!

I love you, I love you,
I love you, I do.
But don't get excited,
I love monkeys, too!

Anonymous

Short Love Poem

It's hard to love
The tallest girl
When you're the shortest guy,
For every time
You try to look
Your true love in the eye
You see
Her bellybutton.

Judith Viorst

11

Captain Soapsuds

My name is Captain Soapsuds—
I rule the waters deep.
When serpents see me coming,
they shudder and they weep.

I'm Captain Suds the pirate,
a mighty ship I sail.
I love to feel the sea mist
and hear the cold wind wail.

I count my bags of treasure.
I make men walk the plank.
I wish I had more fingers
to count the ships I sank.

And if you choose to fight me,
I'll crush you like a bug.
I'm Captain Suds the pirate
till Mommy pulls the plug.

Robert Scotellaro

Swimming Ool

Swimming in the swimming pool
is where I like to "B,"
wearing underwater goggles
so that I can "C."
Yesterday, before I swam,
I drank a cup of "T."
Now the pool's a "swimming ool"
because I took a "P."

Kenn Nesbitt

Dance Fever

Dad's doing a rumba, Dad's doing a waltz,
he's doing a split on the floor.
He's doing a cha-cha across our big couch—
he's prancing right out of the door.

He's doing a polka across the front yard.
He's doing a fox trot, the twist.
He's doing a samba, a tap-dance, ballet—
there isn't a dance step he's missed.

Our father's not noted for moving so fast—
we never have known him to dance.
Yet he's doing a tango, the hula, a jig
since I dropped ice down his pants.

Robert Scotellaro

The Skateboard

My Daddy has bought me a skateboard;
he tried it out first at the store.
And that is the reason why Mommy
says Daddy can't walk any more.

Willard R. Espy

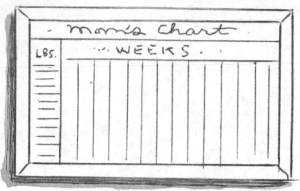

Lost and Not Found

My mom (who's on a diet)
says she's lost another pound.
I've tried to help her find it,
but it's nowhere to be found.

Babs Bell Hajdusiewicz

Mother's Chocolate Valentine

I bought a box of chocolate hearts,
a present for my mother,
they looked so good I tasted one,
and then I tried another.

They both were so delicious
that I ate another four,
and then another couple,
and then half a dozen more.

I couldn't seem to stop myself,
I nibbled on and on,
before I knew what happened
all the chocolate hearts were gone.

I felt a little guilty,
I was stuffed down to my socks,
I ate my mother's valentine . . .
I hope she likes the box.

Jack Prelutsky

The Sleepover

My dad approved an overnight.
I promised we would sleep—
that after ten o'clock at night,
he wouldn't hear a peep.

My friends came over to the house.
They brought their sleeping stuff.
We played full-contact football
till it got a little rough.

We watched some scary movies,
and we had a pillow fight.
We ate too many brownies,
then we joked and teased all night.

My groggy dad came in the room
at three, or was it four?
He found us throwing popcorn—
we were wrestling on the floor.

The promise that I made him
was impossible to keep.
At any decent sleepover,
the point is *not* to sleep!

Betsy Franco

Before 9 A.M.

I brushed my teeth
(and my chin too).
I combed the dog
and tied one shoe.
I hit my brother
(not too hard)
and colored Daddy's
credit card.
I watched cartoons
and wet my clothes.
Then ate some breakfast: —
Oreos.
I built a Lego
centipede,
I washed my Frisbee,
tried to read.
I counted marbles,
played my drum.
I climbed the bookshelf,
sucked my thumb.
I hid a treasure,
drew a map.
Why does Mommy
need a nap?

Joyce Armor

If You Make Me Go to Bed Now

If you make me go to bed now
I am sure that I would hear
The sound of a mosquito
Buzzing loudly in my ear.
So, of course, I'd try to swat him
As I saw him try to land,
But I'd miss and break the bed lamp
And I know I'd hurt my hand,
So I'd need to find some bandages
To help to ease the pain,
But, in the dark, I'd bang my knee
So hard I'd need a cane,
And the ache would be so awful
That I wouldn't sleep a wink,
So I'd go to school next morning
And I couldn't even think,
So of course I'd fail my math test
And my other subjects, too,

I'd be so sad and embarrassed
There'd be nothing left to do
Except run away from home
About as far as I could go,
So I'd limp off to Alaska
And I'd trudge through ice and snow,
Till I met a hungry grizzly bear
All fierce and mean and mad
And as that grizzly ate me . . .
I'd remember Mom and Dad.
Yes, I'd think of my dear parents
And their final words to me,
"Get into bed this minute!
Turn that light off instantly!"

Let this poem be a warning
To all parents everywhere:
If you send your kids to bed,
They may be . . .
Digested by a bear.

Jeff Moss

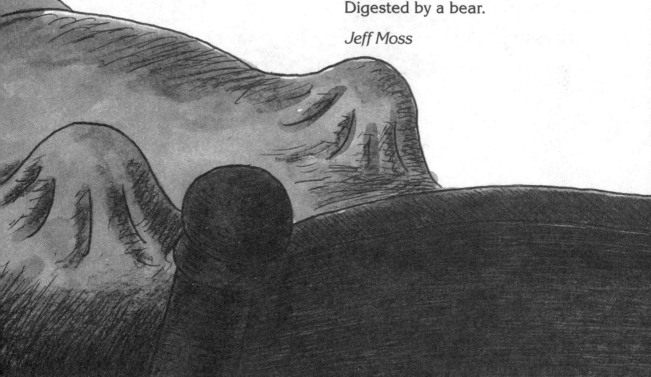

There Was a Man

There was a man who never was.
This tragedy occurred because
His parents, being none too smart,
Were born two hundred years apart.

Dennis Lee

My Baby Brother

My baby brother is so small,
he's hardly even there at all.
The only way that I can find him
is by the smell he leaves behind him.

Bruce Lansky

Babies

That tough western cowboy out herding his cattle
Once lay in his crib with a blankie and rattle.
The TV news lady, though this may seem strange,
Once sat in her diapers and needed a change.
Each major-league ball player once was so small
The one way to get to first base was to crawl,
And even your teacher who's so smart at school
Would lie in her playpen and gurgle and drool.
So love your new sister and please don't forget
Even *you* were once tiny and noisy and wet.

Jeff Moss

My Problem's Worse!

We overslept and missed the bus,
and everybody's in a fuss.
My mom's complaining she'll be late;
she's s'posed to be at work by eight,
and Carla's whining in the back
that no one packed her morning snack,
and Rudy thinks he's got it rough
'cause he forgot his science stuff.
But all their problems can't compare—
at least *they're* wearing underwear!

Babs Bell Hajdusiewicz

31

My Brother

I want to push my brother in a vat of slimy goo.
Or send him in a crate by U.P.S. to Timbuktu.
Perhaps I could place super glue upon his toilet seat.
Or maybe fill his shoes up with fast-drying wet concrete.
Now please don't get me wrong, I really love my brother, Scooter.
But I never ever get a chance to play on our computer.

Luke Havumaki

Things I'm Going to Do to My Brother

First I'm going to tie his shoes
in sixty dozen knots.
Then I'm going to fill his bed
with rotten apricots.
After that I'll get some gum
and squoosh it in his hair,
then put a glob of itching cream
inside his underwear.
I'll pluck his nose hairs one by one
and light them all on fire,
and load his catcher's mitt with glue
and whack him with a tire.
Really, I'll do this and more
(I've got to take a stand).
The next time that my brother snaps
me with a rubber band.

Joyce Armor

My Brother Built a Robot

My brother built a robot
that does not exactly work,
as soon as it was finished,
it began to go berserk,
its eyes grew incandescent
and its nose appeared to gleam,
it bellowed unbenignly
and its ears emitted steam.

My brother built that robot
to help us clean our room,
instead, it ate the dust pan
and attacked us with the broom,
it pulled apart our pillows,
it disheveled both our beds,
it took a box of crayons
and it doodled on our heads.

That robot seemed relentless
as it tied our socks in knots,
then clunked into the kitchen
and dismantled pans and pots,
the thing was not behaving
in the fashion we had planned,
it clanked into the bathroom
and it filled the tub with sand.

We tried to disconnect it,
but it was to no avail,
it picked us up and dropped us
in an empty garbage pail,
we cannot stop that robot,
for we're stymied by one hitch. . . .
my brother didn't bother
to equip it with a switch.

Jack Prelutsky

Potty Trainer

My sister's being potty trained.
I'm really very glad.
'Cause changing diapers isn't fun
and messy pants smell bad.

My mom says, "Won't you help me, dear?"
So I say, "Sure, okay."
(Sometimes I'm rather helpful
in a lazy sort of way.)

But this is unacceptable!
I'm at the baby's feet—
trying everything I can
to keep her on the seat.

I'm reading books; I'm singing songs;
I'm telling stories, too.
The only thing I haven't done
is show her what to do.

Susan D. Anderson

Forgetful

My sister woke up in the morning.
She had to go potty real bad.
I must have forgotten to put the seat down.
She fell in the toilet—how sad.

She yelled and she screamed and she hollered.
There's no doubt that she was upset.
Whenever my sister is nasty to me,
it seems that I always forget.

Bruce Lansky

37

For Sale

One sister for sale!
One sister for sale!
One crying and spying young sister for sale!
I'm really not kidding,
So who'll start the bidding?
Do I hear a dollar?
A nickel?
A penny?
Oh, isn't there, isn't there, isn't there any
One kid who will buy this old sister for sale,
This crying and spying young sister for sale?

Shel Silverstein

School Rules

Do not oversleep and miss the school bus,
you'll be late.
That's a habit teachers generally
don't appreciate.

Never call your teacher a name
when she's not near you.
Teachers' ears are excellent,
so they can always hear you.

Never tell your friends at school
that you still wet your bed.
They are sure to tease you,
and you'll wish that you were dead.

If you go out for a team
it's always wise to practice.
When you are a substitute,
the bench can feel like cactus.

Do not read a textbook when your hands
aren't clean, it's tricky
to separate the pages when the pages
get real sticky.

Never copy homework from a friend
who is a dummy.
If you do, I guarantee
your homework will be crummy.

And if your report card's bad,
don't blame it on your buddy.
Kiss up to your parents quick,
or they might make you study.

Bruce Lansky

No Thanks

I'd rather eat roaches
and grasshopper punch
than try to digest
even one more school lunch.

Joyce Armor

Jasper Jeans

In the lunch room Jasper Jeans
ate twelve helpings of baked beans.
One hour later, filled with gas,
he emptied out our science class.

Russ Walsh

My Feet

My feet, my feet,
I love my feet.
I think they're great,
I think they're neat.

They're pretty, pink,
and picturesque.
They look so perfect
on my desk.

Unfortunately,
sad to tell,
they also have
a funny smell.

So though I'm fast,
and though I'm fleet,
and though at sports
I can't be beat,

no team will pick
me to compete,
because they always
smell defeat.

Kenn Nesbitt

Oops!

Three coffee cups my mother loved
lie shattered on the floor.
Three ripe tomatoes splattered
when they hit the kitchen door.

Three jumbo eggs are scrambled.
But they're not on a plate.
Three loaves of bread are crumbled.
I'll use the crumbs for bait.

Three Barbie dolls have lost their heads.
Three pepper mills are smashed.
Three goldfish died while doing flips.
Three model airplanes crashed.

Three lettuce heads unraveled.
Three onions came unpeeled.
My parents didn't know who did it
till my sister squealed.

My parents are befuddled.
They think that I've gone nuts.
But there's a simpler explanation:
I'm a juggling klutz.

Bruce Lansky

The Proper Way to Eat

The way to eat your lunch meat
is to roll it into tubes.
The way to eat your Jell-O
is to jiggle all the cubes.
The way to eat your Swiss cheese
is to nibble it like mice.

The way to eat your water
is to chew the chunks of ice.
The way to eat your doughnut
is to try to save the hole.
The way to eat your ice cream
is to overfill the bowl.

48

The way to eat your pudding
is to suck it through a straw.
The way to eat your peanuts
is to store them in your jaw.
The way to eat your apple
is to munch it like a hog.

The way to eat your spinach
is to feed it to your dog.
The way to eat your noodles
is in one unending slurp.
The way to end your meal
is with a record-breaking BURP.

John Frank

An "Everything" Pizza

I ordered an "everything" pizza,
which probably was a mistake.
For it came with a bagful of doughnuts;
it came with a shovel and rake.
It came with a woman named Ida.
It came with a man from Peru.
It came with a half jar of peanuts.
It came with somebody's left shoe.
It came with a clown from the circus.
It came with a butterfly net.
It came with a small piece of Kleenex
that was used by Marie Antoinette.
It came with an open umbrella.
It came with some old smelly socks.
It came with a picture of Lassie,
and two lovely grandfather clocks.

It came with a nice set of dishes.
It came with a stale loaf of bread.
It came with a sack of potatoes.
It came with a four-poster bed.
It came with a dining room table.
It came with a washer and dryer.
It came with a broken guitar string.
It came with a radial tire.
It came with a golden retriever.
It came with a basket of fruit.
It came with a bottle of mustard.
It came with a red rubber boot.
It came with a college professor.
It came with a hive full of bees.
And then—this is simply amazing—
they forgot to put on any cheese!

Linda J. Knaus

51

A Balanced Diet

I eat a balanced diet,
I do it day and night—
a pound of brownies on my left,
a pound upon my right.

And filling up my right hand,
with clear and certain heft,
a twelve-ounce bag of jellybeans.
The same is on my left.

A candy cane in one hand,
and likewise in the other.
There are equal sweets on either side,
a big frown from my mother.

I eat a balanced diet,
but mother disagrees.
I just don't understand it.
She's so darned hard to please!

Robert Scotellaro

Big Mary

Mary had a little lamb,
a little toast,
a little jam,
a little pizza
and some cake,
some French fries
and a chocolate shake,
a little burger
on a bun.
And that's why Mary
weighs a ton.

Bill Dodds

Powdered Sugar

I hurried in the restaurant
to have a special treat.
I ordered pancakes covered with
my favorite thing to eat.

It wasn't maple syrup,
not molasses, honey, jam.
I said, "Put heaps and piles
of powdered sugar on it Ma'am."

The food arrived completely coated
with the tasty fluff.
I cut a bite and raised my fork
to gobble up the stuff.

Instead, I goofed—I breathed it in
and quickly had to cough.
My choking blasted
all the luscious
pancake topping off.

54

I blew a powdered sugar storm
that flurried 'round the room.
It snowed on the linoleum—
the waitress got a broom.

It fell on heads like dandruff flakes.
It frosted every light.
It powdered babies' bottoms,
and turned chocolate milk to white.

I blinked, and rubbed my cloudy eyes,
and sneezed a snow-white booger.
I saw my pancakes, and I said,
"I need more powdered sugar!"

Sydnie Meltzer Kleinhenz

Little Miss Muffet

Little Miss Muffet
sat on a tuffet
eating her curds and whey.
Along came a spider
who sat down beside her.
And since she was still hungry,
she ate the spider, too.

Bruce Lansky

56

Cockroach Sandwich

Cockroach sandwich
For my lunch,
Hate the taste
But love the crunch!

Colin McNaughton

57

The Yuckiest Sandwich

Take a slice of moldy bread.
Spread it thick with mud.
Add an onion ring or two,
topped with slimy crud.

Sprinkle fish food all around—
add a dried-up bug.
Smear the whole thing with the lint
you picked up off the rug.

Garnish it with coffee grounds
or hair spray from your mother.
Then wrap it up in cellophane
and give it to your brother!

Ellen Jackson

Table Manners

If I were to make up the etiquette rules,
it wouldn't be too impolite
to reach for the biggest dessert on the tray
and gobble it down in one bite;
to beat on my brother with drumsticks;
eat corn on the cob with my toes;
stand up on my chair and shout, "Food fight!"
hang string beans right out of my nose.

I'd say it's okay to blow bubbles in milk;
to dribble and slobber and slurp;
to yackety-yak with my mouth full of food,
then swallow and let out a burp.
It wouldn't be crude to bounce meatballs,
to hide all the veggies I hate,
stick bubble gum under the table,
or lick all my fingers and plate.

And after I made up the etiquette rules
there's one other thing I would do.
Whenever my parents are eating,
I'd make them obey the rules, too.

Joan Horton

Sound Off!

Our bodies sound off all the time.
What noises we can make!
It happens when we're fast asleep,
or when we're wide awake.

Hands clap and slap, and fingers snap.
We cough and sneeze and snore.
Our hungry stomachs growl for food,
then rumble for some more.

Our feet tap and our bones go pop.
Our lips smack and they slurp.
But most unusual of all
is when our bottoms burp!

Susan D. Anderson

Beans

Beans, beans, the musical fruit,
the more you eat, the more you toot.
The more you toot, the better you feel.
So eat baked beans with every meal.

Anonymous

The Bathroom

My mom calls it the powder room,
my dad calls it the john,
but I call it the stinky room
unless the fan is on.

Babs Bell Hajdusiewicz

64

Sprinkles

If you sprinkle
when you tinkle,
please be neat
and wipe the seat.

Anonymous

65

The Curse of the Foul-Smelling Armpit

The curse of the foul-smelling armpit
is the one thing it's best to avoid;
it's a HORROR that lurks unsuspecting
and has many a friendship destroyed.
For people no longer stand near you—
they throw back their heads in despair
and rush away looking quite frantic,
the shock is just TOO MUCH to bear!

When questioned, nine out of ten people
agreed they would much rather spend
a night in a CREEPY OLD CASTLE
than next to a 'foul armpit' friend!
The president said in the White House,
"It's the very best WEAPON we've got!
Much stronger than onions and garlic,
or cabbages starting to rot!"

If thousands of men with foul armpits
could parachute down from the sky
right onto an enemy army,
they'd force them to curl up and die!
No weapon could match this performance;
we'd win without firing a gun!
Defense cuts would run into BILLIONS—
and fighting a war would be fun!

To people with foul-smelling armpits
the message is clear as can be:
BUY A SPRAY and your friends will be glad that
you don't smell as grungy as me!

Trevor Harvey

6/13/10

I See London

I see London. I see France.
I see _____'s underpants.
       (name)
I can see that they are pink.
But, oh my goodness, do they stink!

Anonymous

My Robot

I have a robot
Do the dishes,
Phone my friends,
Bone the fishes.
Rub my back,
Scrub the floors;
Mop the kitchen,
Open doors.
Do my homework,
Make my bed;
Catch my colds,
Scratch my head.
Walk the dog,
Feed the cats;
Hit my sister,
Knit me hats.

Do my laundry,
Clean my room;
(Boy, he's handy
With a broom).
Comb my hair,
Darn my socks;
Find my lost toys,
Wind my clocks.
Mix me milk shakes,
Fix my bike;
Buy me all
The things I like.
Grill me hot dogs,
Guard my home—
Who do *you* think
Wrote this poem?

Douglas Florian

Miss Veronica Blair

Miss Veronica Blair had long, beautiful hair,
but Veronica hated shampooing it.
She wanted no more of the tedious chore,
so one day she simply stopped doing it.

She piled it instead on the top of her head
back away from her face and her ears,
used a can of hair spray to secure it that way,
and forgot all about it for years.

Well, that did the trick; it got hard like a brick.
She could not hold her head up with ease.
Nor was she aware that the spray in her hair
would be quite so attractive to bees.

They thought it was nectar and came to inspect her.
And soon they were building a hive.
Their numbers increased and grew to at least
three hundred and seventy-five.

They were busy in there, deep inside of her hair.
It must have felt terribly funny.
But bees never rest, as you've probably guessed,
and soon she was dripping with honey.

All sticky and sweet she looked tempting to eat
and was gobbled right up by a bear.
She wouldn't be dead if she'd shampooed her head.
Good-bye Miss Veronica Blair.

Linda J. Knaus

73

Humpty Dumpty's Funeral

At Humpty Dumpty's funeral,
the loss was felt by all,
and everyone was shocked to learn
of Humpty's fatal fall.

They held the funeral in a church.
The guests were all quite sad.
They had to close the casket up
'cause Humpty looked so bad.

The king's best men and horses
couldn't patch old Humpty's crack.
Prince Charming even kissed him,
but he couldn't bring him back.

And Simple Simon sat and sulked.
The blow to him was bitter.
The woman in the shoe stayed home.
(She couldn't find a sitter.)

And Mary had a little lamb
to cuddle as she cried,
but Old MacDonald smelled so gross
he had to stay outside.

The Seven Dwarfs attended too,
and even Happy wept,
but Rip Van Winkle never showed—
he must have overslept.

So Jack and Jill went up the hill
in hopes of fetching him.
Two famous brothers did show up,
and boy, did they look Grimm.

The service was expensive—
they sent Old King Cole the bill.
The Wicked Witch came only
for the reading of the will.

The wall is now off-limits,
and to climb it is a crime.
It's hoped that no more foolish eggs
will go before their time.

Though Humpty was a real good egg,
his future had been spoiled.
As Mother Goose so sadly said,
"He should have been hard boiled."

Blaine and Hardy VanRy

Professor Von Shtoot's Wacky Inventions

Here's a list that proudly mentions
all my wonderful inventions:
older sister shut-her-upper,
all-nutritious chocolate supper,
teacher homework-memory-loss,
potion making you the boss,
baseball bat that never misses,
pin that wards off juicy kisses,
past-your-bedtime length extender,
getting into trouble ender,
vanish cream to use on braggers,
magic dust, defusing naggers,
yucky, mucky meat loaf buster,
out-the-window liver thruster,

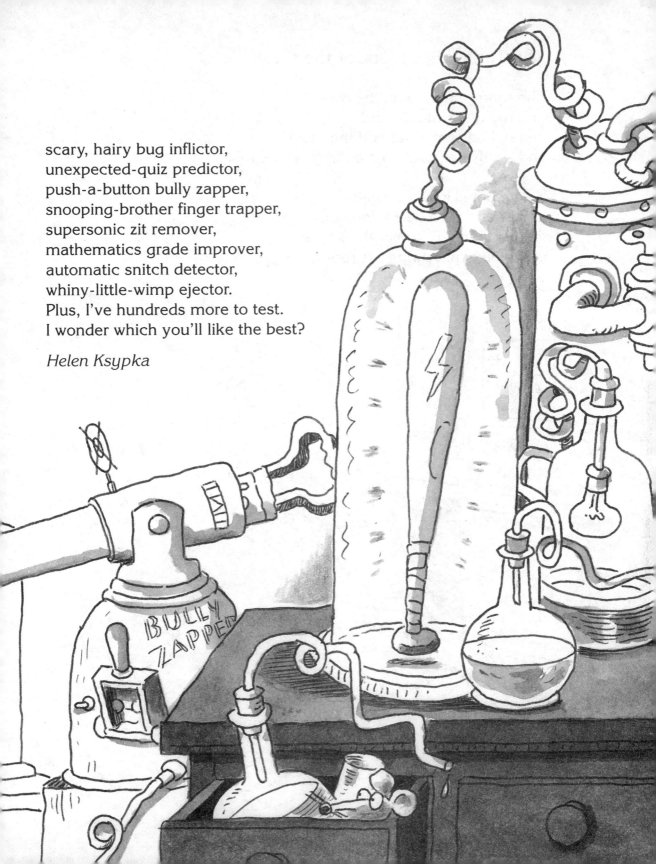

scary, hairy bug inflictor,
unexpected-quiz predictor,
push-a-button bully zapper,
snooping-brother finger trapper,
supersonic zit remover,
mathematics grade improver,
automatic snitch detector,
whiny-little-wimp ejector.
Plus, I've hundreds more to test.
I wonder which you'll like the best?

Helen Ksypka

The Turkey Shot Out of the Oven

The turkey shot out of the oven
and rocketed into the air,
it knocked every plate off the table
and partly demolished a chair.

It ricocheted into a corner
and burst with a deafening boom,
then splattered all over the kitchen,
completely obscuring the room.

It stuck to the walls and the windows,
it totally coated the floor,
there was turkey attached to the ceiling,
where there'd never been turkey before.

It blanketed every appliance,
it smeared every saucer and bowl,
there wasn't a way I could stop it,
that turkey was out of control.

I scraped and I scrubbed with displeasure,
and thought with chagrin as I mopped,
that I'd never again stuff a turkey
with popcorn that hadn't been popped.

Jack Prelutsky

One-Shoe Willy

I stepped in some gum, and I felt really dumb
when my tennis shoe stuck to the street.
I pulled and I tugged, then I hopelessly shrugged
while my face turned as red as a beet.

So I took off my shoe, for what else could I do,
and limped home looking quite pale and ashen.
But lo and behold, the next day I was told
that I'd started a popular fashion.

Linda J. Knaus

80

True Story

This morning I jumped on my horse
And went out for a ride,
And some wild outlaws chased me
And they shot me in the side.
So I crawled into a wildcat's cave
To find a place to hide,
But some pirates found me sleeping there,
And soon they had me tied
To a pole and built a fire
Under me—I almost cried
Till a mermaid came and cut me loose
And begged to be my bride,
So I said I'd come back Wednesday
But I must admit I lied.
Then I ran into a jungle swamp
But I forgot my guide
And I stepped into some quicksand,
And no matter how I tried
I couldn't get out, until I met
A water snake named Clyde,
Who pulled me to some cannibals
Who planned to have me fried.
But an eagle came and swooped me up
And through the air we flied,
But he dropped me in a boiling lake
A thousand miles wide.
And you'll never guess what I did then—
I DIED.

Shel Silverstein

Dinosaur Names

If the dinosaurs had such peanut-sized brains,
why were they given such difficult names?
Why not Beak Mouth or Bonehead or Horny or Chops,
instead of a mouthful like Triceratops?
And as sure as the winged Archaeopteryx flew,
a much simpler name like Fly Guy would do.
If dinosaurs knew that their names were so tough,
they'd turn in their graves and cause earthquakes and stuff!
Why not Spiny or Spike for our friend Stegosaurus?
And Stretch seems to work for the long Brontosaurus.
Their names should be simple and bold and distinct—
I wish that long dinosaur names were extinct!

Holly Davis

My Family of Dinosaurs

My sister, finkasaurus,
is a tattletaling shrew.
My brother, slobasaurus,
doesn't quite know how to chew.
My mother, rushasaurus,
finds it hard to be on time.
My father, cheapasaurus,
never spends an extra dime.
Our doggy, barkasaurus,
keeps the neighbors up at night.
Our kitty, scratchasaurus,
gouges everything in sight.
And then there's angelsaurus—
who, you might have guessed, is me—
the only one who's perfect in this crazy family.

Helen Ksypka

My New Pet

I asked my father for a pet.
He said, "I'll take you shopping."
My father took me to a store
where animals were hopping.

He asked me, "Which one would you like?"
So I picked out a puppy,
a parakeet, a rabbit,
plus a gerbil and a guppy.

I also picked a monkey
and a yellow Siamese cat,
a turtle, snake, and lizard,
plus a very big white rat.

My dad said, "If you want a pet,
then you will have to feed it."
Instead, I picked a storybook.
I cannot wait to read it.

Bruce Lansky

Kangaroos

If a person has four babies
you would call them all quadruplets.
If a kangaroo does likewise
should you call them kangaruplets?

And I've got another question
that could use illuminating:
if a kangaroo is thinking,
is it kangaruminating?

If you baked a kangaroo a pie
and shaped it like a boomerang,
would it be best with whipping cream
or maybe kangaroo meringue?

I've got so many questions,
I just don't know what to do.
I guess perhaps I'll have to go
and ask a kangaroo.

Kenn Nesbitt

Mary's Dumb Lamb

Mary had a little lamb,
'twas awful dumb, it's true.
It followed her across the street
and now it's mutton stew.

Anonymous

Old Hogan's Goat

Old Hogan's goat was feeling fine.
It ate six shirts right off the line.
Old Hogan grabbed him by the back
and tied him to the railroad track.

Now as the train came into sight,
the goat grew pale and green with fright.
It heaved a sigh as if in pain,
coughed up those shirts and flagged the train.

Anonymous

Transylvania Dreaming

In the middle of the night
When you're safe in bed
And the doors are locked
And the cats are fed
And it's much too bright
And sleep won't come
And there's something wrong
And you want your mom
And you hear a noise
And you see a shape

And it looks like a bat
Or a man in a cape
And you dare not breathe
And your heart skips a beat
And you're cold as ice
From your head to your feet
And you say a prayer
And you swear to be good
And you'd run for your life
If you only could

And your eyes are wide
And stuck on stalks
As the thing in black
Toward you walks
And the room goes dark
And you faint clean away
And you don't wake up
Till the very next day . . .

And you open your eyes
And the sun is out
And you jump out of bed
And you sing and shout,

"It was only a dream!"
And you dance around the room
And your heart is as light
As a helium balloon
And your mom rushes in
And says, "Hold on a sec . . .

What are those two little
Holes in your neck?"

Colin McNaughton

93

Hey, Ma, Something's Under My Bed

I hear it at night
when I turn out the light.
It's that creature who's under my bed.
He won't go away.
He's determined to stay.
But I wish he would beat it, instead.

I told him to go,
but he shook his head no.
He was worse than an unwelcome guest.
I gave him a nudge,
but he still wouldn't budge.
It was hard to get rid of the pest.

So I fired one hundred
round cannon balls plundered
from pirate ships sailing the seas.
But he caught them barehanded
and quickly grandstanded
by juggling them nice as you please.

That creature was slick.
He was clever and quick.
This called for a drastic maneuver.
So I lifted my spread
and charged under the bed
with the roar of my mother's new Hoover.

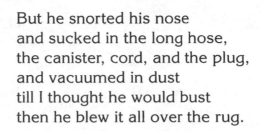

But he snorted his nose
and sucked in the long hose,
the canister, cord, and the plug,
and vacuumed in dust
till I thought he would bust
then he blew it all over the rug.

Now this made me sore,
so I cried, "This is war!"
and sent in a contingent of fleas,
an army of ants
dressed in camouflage pants
followed closely by big killer bees.
But he welcomed them in
with a sly, crafty grin,
and he ate them with crackers and cheese.

I screamed, "That's enough!"
It was time to get tough.
"You asked for it, Creature," I said,
as I picked up and threw,
with an aim sure and true,
my gym sneaker under the bed.

95

With each whiff of the sneaker
the creature grew weaker.
He staggered out gasping for air.
He coughed and he sneezed
and collapsed with a wheeze
and accused me of not playing fair.

Then holding his nose
with his twelve hairy toes,
the creature curled into a ball,
and rolled 'cross the floor
smashing right through the door.
I was rid of him once and for all.

The very next night
when I turned out the light
and was ready to lay down my head,
I heard my kid brother
cry out to my mother,
"Hey, Ma, something's under my bed."

Joan Horton

Mr. Backward

Mr. Backward lives in town.
He never wakes up, he always wakes down.
He eats dessert before his meal.
His plastic plants and flowers are real.
He takes a bath inside his sink
And cleans his clothes with purple ink.
He wears his earmuffs on his nose
And a woolen scarf around his toes.
He loves his gloves worn inside out.
He combs his hair with sauerkraut.
His black dog, Spot, is colored green.
His grandmama is seventeen.
He rakes the leaves still on the trees
And bakes a cake with antifreeze.
He goes to sleep beneath his bed
While wearing slippers on his head.

Douglas Florian

A Sense-less Poem

I'm having trouble with my ears—
they do not see so well.
My eyes are also failing fast—
they've lost their sense of smell.
My nose has lost its power of speech,
my tongue, its sense of touch;
alas, your sympathy's in vain—
my hands can't hear you much.

Carey Blyton

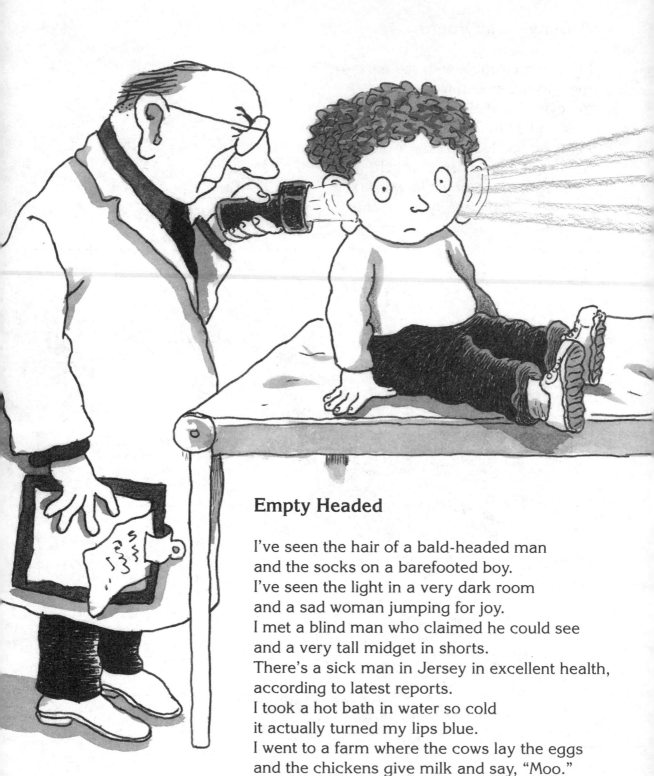

Empty Headed

I've seen the hair of a bald-headed man
and the socks on a barefooted boy.
I've seen the light in a very dark room
and a sad woman jumping for joy.
I met a blind man who claimed he could see
and a very tall midget in shorts.
There's a sick man in Jersey in excellent health,
according to latest reports.
I took a hot bath in water so cold
it actually turned my lips blue.
I went to a farm where the cows lay the eggs
and the chickens give milk and say, "Moo."

I've seen a dead man just barely alive.
I once combed my hair with a brush.
I walked to the store in a taxi one night
to avoid the midafternoon rush.
I sat way up front in the back of the room.
I bought ham that was labeled 'all beef.'
They x-rayed my head and found nothing at all
which I must say is quite a relief.

Linda J. Knaus

Dainty Dottie Dee

There's no one as immaculate
as dainty Dottie Dee,
who clearly is the cleanest
that a human being can be,
no sooner does she waken
than she hoses down her bed,
then hurries to the kitchen,
and disinfects the bread.

She spends the morning sweeping
every inch of every room,
when all the floors are spotless,
Dottie polishes the broom,
she mops the walls and ceilings,
she scrubs beneath the rug,
and should a bug meander by,
she tidies up that bug.

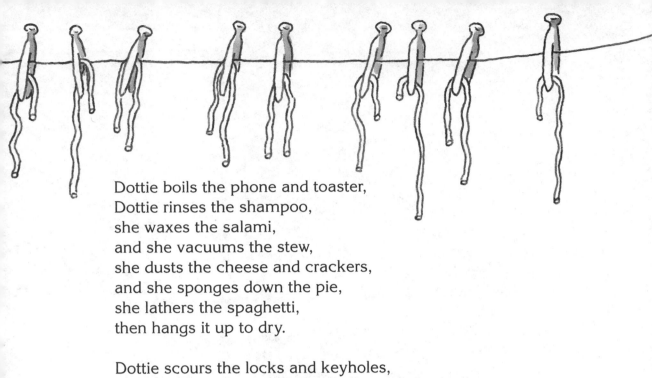

Dottie boils the phone and toaster,
Dottie rinses the shampoo,
she waxes the salami,
and she vacuums the stew,
she dusts the cheese and crackers,
and she sponges down the pie,
she lathers the spaghetti,
then hangs it up to dry.

Dottie scours the locks and keyholes,
and she soaps the bathroom scale,
she launders every light bulb,
she bathes the morning mail,
but her oddest habit ever
(and of this there's little doubt),
is washing all the garbage
before she throws it out.

Jack Prelutsky

The Tattered Billboard

As I was walking down the street
one dark and dreary day,
I came upon a billboard,
and much to my dismay,
the sign was torn and tattered
from the storm the night before.
The wind and rain had done its job
for this is what I saw:

LEARN

in you
Grandm
Underwea

TO PLAY THE PIANO

Smoke Coca-Cola cigarettes,
chew Wrigley's spearmint beer,
Ken-L-Ration dog food
makes your wife's complexion clear.
Simonize your baby
in a Hershey's candy bar,
and Texaco's the beauty cream
that's used by all the stars.
So take your next vacation
in a brand new Frigidaire.
Learn to play the piano
in your grandma's underwear.
Doctors say that babies
should smoke till they are three.
And people over sixty-five
should bathe in Lipton Tea.

Anonymous

Cousin Henrietta's Growing Something On Her Face

Cousin Henrietta's growing something on her face,
just below her pointy nose—it's taking up some space.
Just above her pointy chin, it's growing bigger, stretching.
Come to think about it now I find it rather fetching.
"This is not like Henrietta," Uncle Snipper sighed.
"Look! I think it's growing wider!" Auntie Diddle cried.
Neighbors, friends, and family have gathered by the dozen,
all to see what's growing on our favorite oldest cousin.
What a shock! It's changed her face! We had to stare awhile.
Cousin Henrietta's growing something called a smile.

Jerry Rosen

CREDITS

The publishers have made every effort to trace ownership of the copyrighted material contained in this anthology and to secure all neccessary permission to reprint. In the event that any acknowledgment has been inadvertently omitted, we express our regrets and will make all necessary corrections in future printings.

Grateful acknowledgment is made to the following for permission to reprint the copyrighted material listed below:

Susan D. Anderson for "Potty Trainer" and "Sound Off!" © 1998 by Susan D.Anderson. Used by permission of the author.

Atheneum Books for Young Readers, an imprint of Simon & Schuster Children's Publishing Division, for "Short Love Poem" from *If I Were In Charge of the World and Other Worries* by Judith Viorst. Copyright © 1981 Judith Viorst.

Joyce Armor for "Before 9 A.M.," "No Thanks," and "Things I'm Going to Do to My Brother" © 1998 by Joyce Armor. Used by permission of the author.

Australian Broadcasting Corporation for "A Sense-less Poem" from *Bananas in Pyjamas* by Carey Blyton, published by Faber & Faber. © 1972 by Carey Blyton. Reprinted by permission.

Bantam Books for "If You Make Me Go to Bed Now" and "Babies" from *The Other Side of the Door* by Jeff Moss. Copyright © 1991 by Jeff Moss. Used by permission of Bantam Books, a division of Bantam Doubleday Dell Publishing Group, Inc.

TITLE INDEX

Babies, 28
Balanced Diet, A, 52
Bathroom, The, 64
Beans, 63
Before 9 A.M., 21
Big Mary, 53
Birthday Wish, 4
Born Embarrassed, 2

Captain Soapsuds, 12
Cockroach Sandwich, 57
Cousin Henrietta's Growing
   Something On Her Face, 106
Curse of the Foul-Smelling Armpit,
   The, 66–67

Dainty Dottie Dee, 102–103
Dance Fever, 16
Dinosaur Names, 84
Do Not Enter, 8

Empty Headed, 100–101
"Everything" Pizza, An, 50–51

Forgetful, 37
For Sale, 38

God Gave Out Noses, 3

He'll Pay for This!, 9
Hey, Ma, Something's Under My
   Bed, 94–96
Humpty Dumpty's Funeral, 74–75

I Love You!, 10
I See London, 68
If You Make Me Go To Bed Now, 23
It's Not My Fault!, 6

Jasper Jeans, 43

Kangaroos, 88

Little Miss Muffet, 56
Lost and Not Found, 18

Mary's Dumb Lamb, 90
Miss Veronica Blair, 72–73
Mother's Chocolate Valentine, 19
Mr. Backward, 98
My Baby Brother, 26
My Brother, 32
My Brother Built a Robot, 34

My Family of Dinosaurs, 85
My Feet, 44
My New Pet, 86
My Problem's Worse!, 31
My Robot, 70–71

No Thanks, 42

Old Hogan's Goat, 91
One-Shoe Willy, 80
Oops, 46

Potty Trainer, 36
Powdered Sugar, 54–55
Professor Von Shtoot's Wacky
  Inventions, 76–77
Proper Way to Eat, The, 48

School Rules, 40–41
Self Centered, 7

Sense-less Poem, A, 99
Short Love Poem, 11
Skateboard, The, 17
Sleepover, The, 20
Sound Off!, 62
Sprinkles, 65
Swimming Ool, 14

Table Manners, 61
Tattered Billboard, The, 104–105
There Was a Man, 24
Things I'm Going to Do to My
  Brother, 33
Too Many Birthdays, 5
Transylvania Dreaming, 92–93
True Story, 82
Turkey Shot Out of the Oven, The,
  78–79

Yuckiest Sandwich, The, 58

AUTHOR INDEX

Anderson, Susan D., 36, 62

Anonymous, 3, 7, 10, 63, 65, 68, 90, 91, 104–105

Armor, Joyce, 19, 21, 33, 42

Blyton, Carey, 99

Davis, Holly, 84

Dodds, Bill, 53

Dotlich, Rebecca Kai, 40

Espy, Willard R., 17

Fatchen, Max, 38–39

Florian, Douglas, 70–71, 98

Franco, Betsy, 20

Frank, John, 48

Hajdusiewicz, Babs Bell, 6, 18, 31, 64

Harrison, David L., 9

Harvey, Trevor, 66–67

Havumaki, Luke, 32

Heide, Florence Parry (with Roxanne Heide Pierce), 8

Horton, Joan, 61, 94–96

Jackson, Ellen, 58

Kleinhenz, Sydnie Meltzer, 54–55

Knaus, Linda J., 50–51, 72–73, 80, 100–101

Ksypka, Helen, 76–77, 85

Lansky, Bruce, 2, 5, 26, 37, 40–41, 46, 56, 86

Lee, Dennis, 24

McNaughton, Colin, 57, 92–93

Moss, Jeff, 23, 28

Nesbitt, Kenn, 14, 44, 88

Nicholas, Geraldine, 48–49

Pierce, Roxanne Heide (with Florence Parry Heide), 8

Prelutsky, Jack, 19, 34, 78–79, 102–103

Rosen, Jerry, 106

Scotellaro, Robert, 12, 16, 52

Shore, Diane ZuHone, 4

Silverstein, Shel, 38, 82

Sudol, David, 65

VanRy, Blaine and Hardy, 74–75

Viorst, Judith, 11

Walsh, Russ, 43